UNDERPANTS WONDERPANTS

First published by Parragon in 2013
Parragon
Chartist House
15–17 Trim Street
Bath BA1 1HA, UK
www.parragon.com

Copyright © Parragon Books Ltd 2013

Written by Peter Bently
Edited by Laura Baker
Production by Richard Wheeler

Illustrated by Deborah Melmon
Designed by Ailsa Cullen

ISBN 978-1-4723-1996-8

Printed in China

UNDERPANTS
WONDERPANTS

PaRragon

Bath • New York • Singapore • Hong Kong • Cologne • Delhi
Melbourne • Amsterdam • Johannesburg • Shenzhen

Is it an eagle?

Is it a plane?

NO – it's **underpants wonderpants**
to the **rescue** again!

Whenever you **need** him,

in **sun,**

snow

or **shower,**

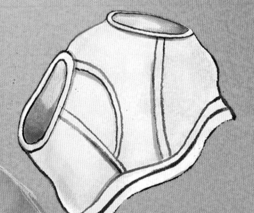

he'll **sort** out your

problems with

UNDERPANTS POWER!

"Elephant **sat** on our nest!"
grumbles Mouse.

"No problem!" says **WONDERPANTS.**

ZAP!

An **underpants** house!

Polar Bear Cub
can't keep up in the **storm**.

ZAP!
Thanks to **WONDERPANTS** she's **cosy**
and **warm!**

Kangaroo cries,
"I've been **itching**
all night!"
ZAP!

In this hammock,
the insects can't **bite!**

The fisherman's
ripped a **big** hole
in his net. ZAP!

"Thank you, **WONDERPANTS!**
It's my **biggest** catch yet!"

"**Help!**" cries the Queen.
It's so far to the ground —

WONDERPANTS' Pantachute helps her land **safe** and **sound!**

Wonderpants zooms to the river, and in a great swoop –

he puts out
the **fire** with his
super-pant-scoop!

But that's not
the **end** of his
super-pants day...

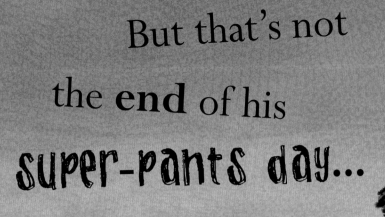

An **alien spaceship** is heading this way!

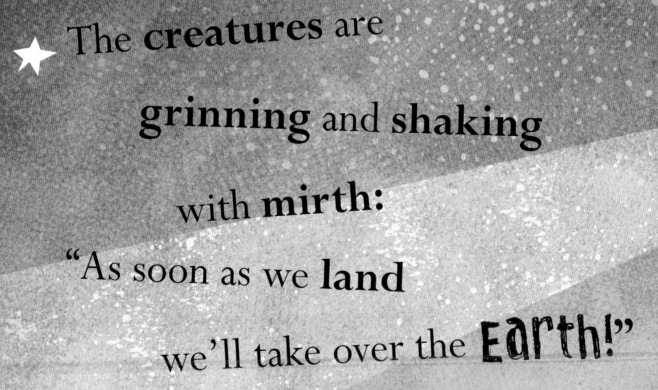

The **creatures** are

grinning and **shaking**

with **mirth:**
"As soon as we **land**

we'll take over the **Earth!**"

But **imagine** the look on
each **alien's** face

when a **Wonderpants**

sling sends them — **ZAP!** — back to **space!**

The people all **cheer**

as they **watch** from afar:

"**Wonderpants**

saved us all —

"He's our
SUPER-PANTS STAR!"